First Summer Romance

First Summer Romance

First Summer Romance

From First Kiss to Eternal Love

Volume 1 of the Immortal Love Series

A Novella

by Olson J. S.

The purpose of copyright is to encourage writers and artists to produce the creative works that enrich our culture.

Cube17, Inc., 4364 Bonita Road No. 241, Bonita, CA 91902

First Edition 2019

Printed in the United States of America

ISBN: 978-0-9821425-9-2

Get the free secret chapters at www.OlsonJS.com

If you only had a day to love,
how would you love?

First Summer Romance

First Summer Romance

Chapter 1: New Friends

Monkey

"I'm going outside," I told my aunt Laura.

"Are you sure? It's one hundred degrees out, you'll melt," she said.

"Yeah, I'm bored. I've been stuck here for almost a week."

"Do you want to play a board game?" Said aunt Laura.

"Not really" I said. "I want to do something else."

"How about we go to the mall?"

"No thanks, I'm going outside," I said, putting on my tennis shoes.

"You don't want to watch another movie? I can make popcorn," she said.

"I'm OK aunt." I said smiling. "You don't have to worry about me. I'm OK."

"Are you sure?" She asked.

"I'm sure." I said. My aunt worries way too much. It's not the first time my mom goes into rehab, but it's the first time she gets arrested. The cops stopped her because she ran a stop sign, and noticed she was high. She was clean for a whole year, but she got fired that day and she couldn't handle it. She used heroine. It was all my fault.

I ran out. The sun pinched my skin as soon as I closed the door behind me. It took me a moment to readjust to the light. I turned left and right to figure out where I was according to the buildings around me. I started my way walking through the apartment buildings, trying to stay in the shade as much as possible. I moved slowly, exploring every alley and climbing every tree. It was not as boring as being stuck at the apartment, but it wasn't a great adventure either.

The next day I would make a plan of attack, starting by climbing the large trees I found a few buildings away, and then going into the community pool every hour to cool down. Today I would find the tallest tree and climb it. Then the pool to cool off.

I was a good climber. As thin and light as a twig, I could pull myself up high up the trees and the branches could hold my weight. I found my tree. Taking a running start, I kicked off the trunk, jumping into the second branch. It was a large branch, thicker than my leg. I pulled myself up and sat there looking up, devising the best path to the top. *Channel the monkey*. It's an old trick I use to channel whoever I needed for the task. I did this all the time. When I'm practicing martial arts I say, "Channel a Shaolin Monk." When I'm getting creative or want to solve a problem I channel Einstein. Today it was my old friend Monkey. I've channeled him before. I started my way up, making sure each branch could hold me. It was easy. I got half way up when I suddenly heard a voice.

"How did you get up so high?" I looked down, spotting two boys.

"Are you like a monkey?" The smaller boy asked.

I started making monkey noises and scratching my ribs, belly and armpits. "Uh uh uh ah ah ah," I belched.

They laughed, looking at each other pointing at me. "He's like a monkey," said the small one.

"I want to get up," the older boy said, moving closer to the trunk of the tree.

"You have to jump and grab the first branch, then pull your leg over it and turn your body," I told him.

The taller boy jumped and got ahold of the branch but could not do anything. He was just hanging on.

"Pull yourself up," I told him while I climbed down a bit.

"I can't," he said.

"I'll go down and help you," I said. I climbed down, jumping off the last branch. I think they were impressed. "Jump and get your leg up like this." I demonstrated how to do it. "I'll push you up." He jumped and I pushed his hips until his leg wrapped around the branch. Then I pushed him up onto the branch.

"Now me," said the smaller boy.

"OK, can you reach the branch?" I asked.

He jumped up but could not even touch the branch. He tried again. Nothing. "He doesn't know how to jump," said the other boy.

"Everyone knows how to jump," I said. "Not him," he shook his head.

"I can carry you," I told him as I stood under the branch. "Come here," I said. He did as I asked and reached up with both hands. I squatted and grabbed both his legs while carrying him up to reach the branch, then I pushed his hips up like I did with his brother and helped him turn to get up and on the branch.

"Yes," he said in triumph.

I could have carried them and pushed them onto the branch, but they would never learn how to do it. "This way you can do it on your own next time," I told them.

"Now we know how to do it, Monkey," said the older boy.

"Come on let's climb up," I said, jumping to the first branch.

They followed me to the higher branches and secured themselves next to me with a giant smile.

"What are your names?" I asked them.

"My name is Carlos, I'm ten and that's my little brother Johnny, he's six. What's your name? Are you new here? Do you have brothers?" Carlos asked all at once.

"You can call me Monkey," I said.

"That's not your name," he laughed.

"It's just a nickname," I said.

"Ok Monkey," Carlos said.

"Are you new here?" he asked.

"Yes, I'm new but I'm here only for a few weeks. I don't have any brothers."

"Do you have any sisters? We have a sister; her name is Alma, she's older than us, she's older than you. I bet she could climb this tree," said Carlos.

"That's great," I said.

"So, do you have sisters?" Carlos asked.

"No, I don't."

"So, you are all alone all the time?" Carlos asked in disbelief.

"I guess so," I said.

"Who plays with you?" Carlos asked.

"I play alone most of the time," I answered.

"That's strange." Carlos looked at Johnny, who shrugged.

"I guess that's ok," said Johnny.

"Want to go to the pool?" Carlos asked.

"Now that's what I'm talking about," I said. Finally, I had someone to play with.

"Let's go get Alma. We're not allowed to go into the pool by ourselves. We could drown," said Carlos.

14

"OK," I said.

Chapter 2: Good Morning Sunshine

Alma

Splash! "Damn it, boys." I fell into the toilet again. "What the fuck!" They didn't even flush. I grabbed the sides of the toilet and pushed myself up and out, my butt dripping. Yuk! I flushed and jumped into the shower to wash the pee off. Little did I know this wasn't the only surprise I would have today. Not even close.

After taking way too long in the shower, I walked to my room and dressed for a lazy summer day at home. Old shorts and my comfy Queen cutout t-shirt. It was my Mom's. I found it in her closet with moth holes, so I cut the bottom and the sleeves out, and now it's my favorite. I just wear it around the apartment or when I go to the pool. I wouldn't wear something like that to school. Don't get me wrong, it's a super cool vintage concert t-shirt, but you can see my bellybutton.

I cranked the radio to the classic rock station to opaque the air conditioner humming at full blast. I felt like a butterfly today, so I searched for my Mom's oversized butterfly earrings. The colorful butterflies flapped under my ears. I looked in the mirror, shaking my head to make them wiggle. "Wow!" I got the strongest feeling of *déjà vu.* A tingly sensation went through my whole body. Like a mild electric shock, or what you feel after your leg falls asleep. It went away after a few seconds. "That was so weird."

Drying my hair with the blow dryer always takes too long but I do it anyway. I have way too much hair, long and think, it cascades down my back to my waist like a red cape. Don't get me wrong, I like my bright red hair, even if everyone makes fun of it in school. Maybe I'm just afraid of cutting it. It's been long for so many years that I'm not sure if I'm really me without it.

I walked to the kitchen and decided to make myself another cup of coffee. No sugar, no milk—black like my soul. I searched for my novel while the coffee maker filled the room with my favorite aroma. I crashed back on the couch with my book. *It's way too quiet,* I thought, looking around at the tiny living room. Wouldn't you know it, like clockwork, the door swung open and my two little buggers rushed in, making a ruckus.

"Hey, you have to flush after you go to the bathroom," I said.

"Let's go to the pool," they cried out.

"Right now?" I said, salivating over my half-read book.

"Yes pleeeeeeease!" they said.

"OK then, let's change." I gave in, closing my book and putting it down on the couch. So much for my quiet time.

"What are you drinking?" Carlos said, stopping dead on his tracks.

"Coffee," I said looking at my "I love Mom" mug.

"Since when do you drink coffee?" he asked with his mini attitude.

"Silly boy," I said. I thought about it for a second. Didn't I drink coffee? "I love coffee. Did I drink coffee yesterday?

"C'mon go change," said Carlos.

"We have a new friend." Johnny pointed his finger towards the door.

"Oh yeah?" I got up from the couch, walking towards my bedroom to change.

"Yeah, he's going with us to the pool," continued Johnny.

I decided not to change, putting my bathing suit under what I was already wearing before grabbing my sunglasses from the kitchen table. The boys ran out as fast as they ran in. Seems they made a mess just by passing by. "Don't forget the sunblock." I said while spraying some all over, struggling to get some on the back of my shoulders. I stuck my wallet in my back pocket and strolled out, closing the door behind me.

"This is him." The boys pointed and grinned like, well, little kids. When I turned I saw a boy standing there in front of my door.

"He can climb a tree better than you," said Johnny.

"Ah," I whispered.

"He's like a monkey. He said we should call him Monkey, for real," he said.

"Mmmm," I murmured.

I couldn't help but smile. He was easy on the eyes. I peeked over my sunglasses so I could take a looksee. "Well hello, Monkey," I said, giving him my best devilish smile. I immediately pushed my sunglasses back up with my index finger. The sun was roasting and I could already feel it pinching my skin, especially my arms and legs. Good thing I was wearing sunblock. I super freckle out all over my body with any hint of sun. Not very sexy. I hate my freckles, they make me look polka dotted.

19

The boy stood like a statute, eyes almost popping out of his head like that cartoon. He took a long, slow, detailed scan, starting at my ankles and stopping at my bellybutton. He wasn't particularly smooth about it, either. I waited, striking a pose with one hand on my hip and the other across my stomach. I looked down at my super short shorts. Maybe I should change. Nonsense, we were going to the pool. Wait, I had a bikini under this. I really didn't want to wear a bikini with this pervert around. I paused for a second... no. I didn't have anything else to wear, and I didn't want him to think I changed just for him.

"Hey, Monkey, eyes up here," I said pointing at my eyes with two fingers. He quickly looked up at me. Boys!

"Good morning sunshine," he finally said, looking up at me, with a crooked smile.

At least he was funny. Nice twist to the summer vacation monotony.

"Let's go, let's go," said Johnny running shirtless passed me, a towel over his shoulder.

"I'm Alma," I said, extending my hand.

"I know," he responded, taking an awkward step to shake my hand.

The boy didn't have a towel. "You don't need a towel," I said. "With this sun, we'll dry up in forty-seven seconds." He nodded.

"You have a bathing suit under those shorts?" I asked, looking at his shorts, noticing scrapped, dingy knees.

"No," he said, looking down at them as if noticing them for the very first time. "They double as a swimsuit," he said.

I guessed the boy was eighteen years old like me, almost my height. Finally! I didn't have to feel like the jolly green giant. He was also kind of cute. I took a peek at him again, my eyes lingering on him, but looking away before he noticed. OK, he was too cute. His disheveled, just-out-of-bed brown hair over his young brown eyes and permanent grin gave him the happy, careless look that springs of future confidence. He was skinny, like me, but with scraped knees and elbows. "I like your shirt," I commented.

"It's Return of the Jedi," he said.

Ok, he was also a nerd.

You could hear all the air conditioners from all the apartments in the complex hauling at full speed. It was probably close to one hundred degrees. "So, what's your name?" I asked as we strolled towards the pool.

"Monkey," he said with a childish grin.

I gave him a flirtatious push. "No, it's not," I said.

His smile got wider. "Yes, my real name is Monkey," he said nodding.

"Is that your first name or your last name?" I asked.

"It's my secret agent name," he said.

"Are you trying to be funny?" I asked. "Because you're not succeeding."

"What happened to your shirt?" He asked pointing at it, changing the subject.

"It tried to be funny but didn't succeed. So, I cut it with scissors." I said.

"Oh, no" he exclaimed. "Where are those scissors?"

"Today is your lucky day," I said. "I left them at home."

"So, who is Queen?" He pointed at my t-shirt.

"What?" I stopped in my tracks. "You don't know who Queen is?" I threw my hands up in the air. His face looked terrified. I might have screamed a bit.

"Relax," he said, "I know who Queen is. It's my Mom's favorite band of all time. Well, next to The Beatles."

"Don't joke about music," I said. "It's a deal breaker."

"Deal!" he said, then spit on his hand and extended it.

"Yuck," I said, pulling my hand away, "you're gross."

Monkey and the boys walked with me towards the pool. The boys ran in front of us. I was barefoot and had to jump the boiling concrete sidewalks. He jumped them too, even though he had shoes on. He was funny. I felt a familiar laugh, like I knew him. Like an old friend or something. We opened the gate to the pool and my brothers were already there screwing around. "Don't run," I told them as Carlos ran and dove into the pool.

Just another day in paradise, right? Not. This day would change me, transform me, open my eyes to who I really was.

Chapter 3: The Butterfly Effect

Alma

Monkey took his shoes and socks off. "Who wears socks in the summer?" I thought. He burned his feet on the hot cement. I tried to cover up a laugh. "Rookie," I said as he jumped to stand on his shoes.

He made a funny face. "I did that on purpose," he said grinning.

I unbuttoned and unzipped my shorts, they unwillingly let go of my hips and fell to the floor. I paused for two seconds, then lifted my arms, taking off my top. I could hear his jaw drop to the floor. "Oh my god," he said between his teeth. He wouldn't stop staring, and I wasn't sure if I should cover myself or what. Instead I picked up my shorts and folded them neatly on the chair with my t-shirt. He was still glaring.

This bikini was way too tight, I instantly felt self-conscious. It was from last year and I grew, well, everywhere. Plus, it had yellow polka dots, not very grown up. I turned away to adjust my top, making sure it was covering everything, or at least the important parts. I turned to catch him looking at my bottom. "Show's over," I said.

He pretended he wasn't looking while trying to take his t-shirt off. He pulled it up over his head too quickly and it got stuck; he struggled clumsily. *Yummy.* Boyfriend had some abs on him.

He finally managed to get the t-shirt off and threw it on a chair. Didn't fold it or anything. He turned to see me staring. "What?" he asked.

"Smooth," I said.

"What?" he repeated shrugging his shoulders.

He was probably an athlete. Lean muscles hiding under that loose t-shirt. I colored him up and down as a butterfly hatched in my belly flapping her wings. I touched my stomach to stop it. It didn't work.

"What's up with the six pack?" I asked ignoring the butterfly.

He looked awkward. Didn't know what to say or how to stand. He crossed his arms.

"So, how did you get them?" I pointed at his abs.

"Why?" he asked.

"I just want to know," I said. "Or is it a secret?"

"No, it's not a secret. Just crunches," he said.

"So, you just do crunches to get a six pack? I bet it's to impress the ladies," I pressed. "You're so vain." I shook my head disapprovingly.

"No, I'm not!" he said defensively. "They come with sports," he claimed.

"I'm glad I'm the first girl to see your abs," I said smiling.

"Who said you're the first one?" He tried to comeback. It was a poor showing. I could see right through him.

Maybe he was younger than I had initially thought. "How old are you?" I asked.

"You mean in monkey years?" he asked avoiding the question.

"You're so innocent," I told him smiling, with a bit of attitude.

"So where did you get those giant teeth?" He lashed out.

"Don't be so sensitive," I told him.

"What?" He said, shrugging his shoulders.

I stuck my tongue out at him. "I don't love you anymore," I said.

"Yes, you do," he said running away, jumping in the pool.

We played Marco Polo with the boys and dived for pennies. The kids loved him. It was like he was one of them. "Let's race," said Johnny. We all went to one side of the pool and held on to the edge. "Ready?" I said, "On three; one, two, three." We all sprinted across the pool. We were the only ones there. I swam as fast as I could and popped my head up. Monkey came in after.

"Wow, you're fast," he said. "Again?"

"Alright," I said. We raced again. I got in first again. Monkey laughed. I spit over the edge. Monkey copied me.

"Race under water?" said Monkey.

We raced across the pool again underwater, then backstroke. "Wow! You win again," he said. He was a surprisingly graceful loser. My eyes stung from the chlorine and my fingers were turning into prunes.

It was so much fun. I didn't usually hang out with boys or girls my age. Teenagers were stupid! Boys just wanted one thing. Girls my age are super bitches, superficial and dramatic. This boy was different. I couldn't

27

stop staring at him. Did he notice? I didn't want to be so obvious. "Boyfriend is gorgeous," I thought, the flutter in my belly returning. Did he like me?

Hours went by in seconds, it was getting late and I knew I had to go back to the apartment, feed my brothers and put them to bed. I didn't want this day to end. "My Mom will be back soon," I told him. He nodded. His aunt showed up at the pool soon after, looking for him.

"Hello Aunt Laura," he said to her.

"I think it's time," she said. "Hello Alma how are you," said Laura.

"I'm fine," I said waving. "Boys, say hello to Laura."

"Hello," said the boys. "Do we have to go? Can we stay two more hours?"

"Two more hours?" said Laura Del Mar. "I don't think so. The pool will close soon, and it's late anyway."

"You didn't tell me Laura was your aunt." I said.

"It never came up," he said, "looks like you know her."

"Yea, she's my Mom's friend," I said flicking some water at him. "They play cards every week."

"Let's go kids," said Laura Del Mar, "Your Mom told me to tell you dinner is almost ready."

Ok, so my Mom knows I'm at the pool with a boy. We got out and dried off. Monkey was dripping all the way back. "You can use my towel," I said.

"No, it's fine," he said, walking with his shoes on one hand.

My brothers ran in front of us, as usual. I had so much fun I didn't want the day to end. I felt like I knew this boy. It was an instinct. "So, your last name is Del Mar?" I said.

"Maybe," he said.

"I'll call you Monkey of the sea," I said.

"You speak Spanish," he said. "I'm impressed."

"You impress easily," I said. He pretended to pinch my elbow.

"I had a lot of fun," he said.

"Meet you back at the pool in an hour?" I asked touching his shoulder, leaning in to whisper. He smelled of chlorine.

"It's already nine," he said, trying to whisper.

I put a finger on my lips. "Don't be a baby," I said. "It's summer vacation." He gave me two very awkward thumbs up with a sideways wink.

"Is that a yes?" I whispered, making sure.

He looked at his thumbs perplexed, making a face "That's a double yes," he said.

"OK, I'll take the pool gate key as they close it at nine. If you get there before, wait for me outside." I got another thumbs up.

I got home, and my Mom was making pasta with her special meat tomato sauce. I could hear the ground beef sizzling as the oregano entered my nostrils. "Hi Mom," I said, kissing her on the cheek. My brothers ran into the kitchen giving Mom a great big hug. "We have a new friend and we played all day in the pool…" they told her all about it.

"Was that Laura outside with you just now?" asked Mom, standing over the stove. "Yes," I said walking into the kitchen. "Was that her nephew?" she asked. "Yes," I said grabbing forks, then plates. Mom lifted her gaze to assess my reaction. I pretended not to see her while I set the table.

"I'm starving," said Carlos.

"I'm starving more," said Johnny.

We all sat down around our old scratched wooden table. "Here you go," I said, "a supersized portion, since you guys swam so much today." I served myself a small portion and ate as fast as I could to beat my brothers to the shower. "You're hungry today," said Mom. "Yeah," I said, mouth full. I left the table on my last bite and put my dish in the sink. "I'll wash the dishes later," I said, leaving the kitchen.

"You're in a hurry," said Mom, turning back to see me. I grabbed two white towels. "I'm going to shower," I said before she could get another word out.

I jumped in the shower and prepared to shave my legs. How exciting! I wasn't very hairy, but I had some red fuzz all around my legs. I stared apprehensively at my Mom's old-fashioned razor, the one with a two-sided blade. I didn't want to cut myself, so I took it nice and easy. I soaped up my legs first, then sat on the floor with the razor in my right hand. It wasn't hard. The soap did most of the work. I got up and washed my hair really fast. I did take more time doubling up on the conditioner. The chlorine from the pool was horrible for my hair. All done. Dried off my legs, body and back in one swift motion, wrapped a towel around my hair and put on my Mom's bathrobe. There was no time to dry my hair, so I would dry it when I got back. I didn't like going to bed with damp hair.

I went to Mom's vanity looking for some lipstick and maybe even a bit of her perfume. I've never used make-up and I don't know why I wanted to use it now. It seemed important for the first time. I found a light pink lipstick in the top drawer. "Perfect." I got close to the mirror. "Ah, these freckles!" They were popping up by the hundreds. That's what I got for staying out in the sun too long.

"I see you shaved your legs," Mom said from the doorway.

"Ah, yeah," I said surprised. "Busted."

"This has to be some special boy," she said.

"Not really," I lied.

"Lipstick," she said. "Wow, you're going all out." She looked so beautiful when she smiled. I just stood there grinning.

"It's getting late," she said. "This is no time to go out."

"What?" I was about to start arguing.

"I'm kidding," she said laughing.

"So, tell me about this boy," she said coming into the bedroom. "You ignore all the boys from school and now you're wearing lipstick?"

"I know," I said, not hiding my excitement. "He's funny and witty. He must read a lot because he's smart. I mean, he's a perv since he just stares at me, but I guess it's ok, he's a teenager. But it's so cute the way he does it. I kind of stare at him too. It's just that I'm coy about it. He's nerdy and doesn't care. He's not like the boys from school. He tries to be cool but it's so funny, because he's not…" I rambled on and on, but didn't tell her about his abs.

Mom took a small bag form the vanity, "Come here," she said, motioning me toward her. We sat on her bed. "Let me put on your lipstick." She took a very thin brush from the bag. "Close your mouth," she said, while brushing my lips. She then fetched her eyeshadow palette from the vanity.

"That's too much, Mom. I don't want him to think I'm too eager," I said.

My Mom chuckled. "Trust me, honey. I'll just do a little trick over and around your eyes. They will pop." She took a dark pencil and drew around my eyes, then took another brush. "Close your eyes," she said while applying some color over my eye lids.

"Mom, he's polite and decent. I feel as if we grew up together, as if we're soul mates," I said.

Mom smiled a wide smile. "Where is this hot date taking you?" she asked.

"It's not a date, Mom, we're going to hang out by the pool and just talk."

"The pool is closed at this time," Mom said.

"We're not going to swim," I said. "We're just going to hang out."

"I guess that's ok," Mom said, "just don't leave the complex."

"I know," I said.

"Are you going to kiss him?" she asked pretending to check my makeup.

"Mom?! What kind of question is that?" I cried.

"Well did you think about it?" she asked.

"I thought about it," I answered.

"And?" Mom asked.

"If he tries to kiss me I won't put up a fight," I said giggling.

"What are you wearing?" she asked.

"Just my cut-out jeans and my silver tank top. It's hot outside," I said.

"All right," she said, not sounding very convinced.

"What?" I asked.

"Nothing," she said. "Why not your white mini with your new top?"

"Mom! We're just going to the pool," I said.

I dressed fast in shorts and my silver tank top. "Should I wear a hair clip?" I asked Mom, clipping two on my sides.

"No" she said. "Just leave it straight."

"But it's wet," I said.

"My darling. He won't be looking at your hair," she said, looking me over.

"Mom! Are you trying to pimp me out?" I asked.

"I'm just kidding," she said. 'It's just that I'm so excited. This is the first time you've even talked about a boy without the word stupid attached."

"OK I'm leaving now," I said.

Mom looked at me up and down. "Go rub some baby oil on those legs," she said. "They look so dry."

"But they'll be all shiny," I said.

"Go rub on some baby oil," Mom pointed to the bathroom.

I did as she said.

"Be back by eleven thirty," she said.

"Mom, that's way too early. It's summer break," I protested.

"Don't make me go get you."

"I'm leaving," I said, looking at my Seiko.

"What are the three rules?" my mom asked behind me.

"Mom, I have to go," I said.

"The three rules," she said.

"Don't leave the apartment complex, no drugs, don't get pregnant," I repeated in a robotic voice.

Chapter 4: Kind of a First Date

Alma

I got to the pool and he wasn't there. Had he left already? Maybe he wasn't allowed out so late.

I looked for a good spot away from the unflattering old lamp post and dipped my feet in the lukewarm pool. It was hot and I felt a thick drop of sweat escape from my armpit and . Did I forget to put on deodorant? I looked around and then smelled my armpits. Oh no, I saw him approaching.

"Hey Monkey. Cool hair," I said. He touched it self-consciously.

"Hey," he nodded strolling over, sitting too close.

He stared at me intensely under a ray of moonlight, his gaze penetrating, as if he wanted to take a bite. The butterflies were back, running amuck all around my stomach.

"Your aunt gave you a hard time about going out?" I asked to steady myself.

"No, not really," he said.

He looked at me for too long and looked away. I tucked my hair behind my ear and swallowed, thinking of what to say next. It was quiet, except for the humming of hundreds of air conditioners going at full blast. There was nobody in sight, everyone probably hiding from the heat.

"Do you like school?" I asked.

"Not so much," he said. "I bet you have a 4.0 GPA." he asked.

"Four point five," I said.

"How is that even possible?" He said, "It's like getting one hundred and ten percent on a test with one hundred questions."

"Well it's not the same," I said, "you earn extra credit that raises your GPA. If you already have a four, you get a higher GPA."

"I don't like school much. It's boring and lame. I ditch it all the time," he said.

"What do you mean you ditch? Don't you want to go to college?" Boy, I sound judgmental.

"Yeah, I'll get into college, but I'm not going to just go to class to get the teacher enough students to keep his job. The teacher doesn't care about me, so I don't really care about his class," he said.

That was a deal breaker for me. I didn't want to hang around a dummy. "How will you get into college if you skip class?" I pressed, getting annoyed.

"I'll get into college, it's not that hard," he said.

"What!? You need good grades, a good SAT score, and that doesn't even guarantee you'll get in." This guy might be like all other dumb boys.

"I'll get into community college first, then I'll transfer. Everyone gets into community college," he said.

"Don't you think that's kind of mediocre?" I said. "Just passing by?"

"Just because you find meaning in school doesn't mean it's important," he said, making me furious. "It's just high school. It's a scam left over from the industrial revolution. I way to train farmers into factory workers." He splashed me with some water. I got some in my eye.

"Hey, don't," I said.

"Get over yourself." He splashed again, even more. He got my t-shirt wet. I immediately felt it sticking to my chest. I pinched it and pulled to make sure it wasn't exposing my breasts. Not that there was much to see.

"Stop it," I screamed, slapping his hand hard.

39

He stopped. "Sorry," he said holding his wrist.

"Did I hurt you?" I asked, already regretting screaming, and hitting him so hard.

"It's ok," he said, letting go of his wrist. "I was just playing."

A lump got stuck in my throat. "I know, I'm not used to playing around," I told him. "Sorry I hit you."

"I'll take it as a love bite." He grinned, holding his wrist again.

"I did hurt you," I said, grabbing his hand.

"Don't bite it," he said, pulling away.

"Give it to me." I gestured with my hand. He did, and I rubbed to make the pain go away. He looked at me while I did it—it wasn't an innocent look.

"I don't skip all the time. It's not easy to skip," he said, going back to the subject. "You have to plan it in advance."

"Yeah, how?" I asked, not letting go of his hand.

"Well, you need to know what phone number they'll call to notify your absence. You need to control that voice mail. The school calls my house, and there's nobody there during the day. You also need to know where you're going. I mean, you can't just go to the parking lot. I like going to the movies," he explained. "For that you need to know the movie schedule, if the teachers will be suspicious, and what you'll do if you get caught. If you can't do the time, don't do the crime."

"Seems like you're a little mastermind," I said.

"Yes, otherwise you get caught," he said seriously. "I only do it once or twice per month and I don't ditch the entire day, maybe the last two periods or something like that. I also plant the seed long before. I tell the teacher I have to do something that day. That way they expect my absence."

"Oh my god, you're a hoodlum," I said. "You're not as innocent as you look."

"Who said I looked innocent?" he said.

How adorable.

"So, are you staying here for the summer?" I asked.

"Not sure, maybe longer." He said.

"How long?" I asked with high expectation.

"Don't know." He shifted uncomfortably shrugging his shoulders. His expression got grim.

"Did something happen?" I asked.

His eyes watered. "Kind of," he said.

"What happened?" I asked holding his hand between both of mine.

He took a deep breath. "It's ok. My mom got arrested."

A gasp left my lips unexpectedly.

"It's not the first time," he said, "it's just that she was doing so well, and this time it was kind of my fault."

"What do you mean it was your fault?" I asked.

He hesitated. "Well, I kind of got into a fight at school."

"You kind of got into a fight?" I asked.

"There is this kid Joel. He's my friend, he's super nice and super smart, but some kids make fun of him when I'm not around," he said.

"Why do they make fun of him?" I asked.

"Because they're bullies and stupid, and they only pick on the kids that don't fight back," he said annoyed.

"I see," I said.

"He's also autistic," he said.

I nodded in understanding.

"This time they went too far," he said, "they pushed him to the floor during PE and took his shorts and underwear."

"What did you do?" I asked squeezing his hand.

"I didn't see what happened," he said," I was on the other side of the track. When I got to Joel and saw what happened I saw one of the kids run with Joel's shorts, so I ran after him."

"Yes," I said eyes wide.

"He ran away off the track towards the classrooms. I caught him half way and tackled him."

"Did you hit him?" I said.

"I was so angry," he said, eyes watering, "how can they do that? It wasn't even fair. I found out four of them held him down while this other kid took his shorts."

"What happened?" I asked.

"After I tackled him I sat on top and punched him. He started bleeding, I mean, a lot of blood. Turns out I broke his nose. He was a mess, I got blood all over my shorts and shirt. It looked worse than what it was. I only hit

43

him once." He took a deep breath. "They made such a big deal. They called the police and my mom. She had to leave her job to rush to school and they later fired her. She said they were just looking for an excuse to let her go."

"Did you explain what the other kids did?" I said.

"Yes," he said. "I explained it, Joel explained it, all the other kids told the principal how the kids are super bullies and they always do this kind of stuff. The principal wanted nothing of it. He said it was my fault for hitting the kid."

"That's typical," I said, "This is why bullies don't stop. The school does nothing, and if you try to stop them, then you get in trouble."

"That's exactly what happened," said Monkey.

"But how did your mom get arrested?" I asked.

"My mom had a problem with pain medication," he said. "It started after her car accident, then it became an addiction and she went to jail for stealing. When you're on drugs you'll do anything. She drove around looking for bicycles left out on the driveway, and pawned them for quick cash to get high. She got caught and went to jail but got out on a special probation program. They randomly test her to see if she's still clean. She failed last time and the sheriff came and cuffed her in front of me. It was horrible. My mom is good, she's just sick. This stuff is an illness."

"Where's your mom now?

"She has to stay in jail for three months." He said.

"I see," I said looking at him. "You know there is absolutely no way this is your fault, right?"

"If I hadn't hit the boy," he started saying.

"No," I interrupted, "that's not how it works. I'm sorry, but your mom has other problems that are not related to you. Like you said, it's an illness. You didn't give her the illness, right?"

"No," he admitted.

"I think you have to focus on your mom, not on you, if you want to help her. It's not about you, Monkey," I told him with a smile.

"It's just that she was doing so good," he said.

"Yes, and I'm sure she'll do better when she goes out and you're there to support her," I told him.

"Anyway," he said. "I'm staying with my aunt until my mom is released. We lost our apartment, so we'll look for a new place to stay."

"Maybe you can move in with your aunt, it would be great. You can see me every day."

"How is that so great?" He said grinning.

"Are you pretending to get hard to get? Cause you suck at it," I told him, pushing him with my shoulder.

"That is an option," he said, "my aunt offered. She's so worried about mom. She cries every night when she thinks I can't hear her."

I didn't know what to say to that.

"So, what's your favorite subject?" I asked.

"You," he said with piercing eyes. The tingles in my belly increased. Butterflies.

"No silly. In school," I said, blushing for the first time, like, ever. Could he see me blush under this light? I reached for the ends of my hair.

He thought for a few seconds, looking at the pool. "I like world religions," he said.

"World religions? I don't believe you. You're not in college," I said.

"I don't have it at my school," he said. "I just read it on my own. I also watched all the videos and recorded courses from the library."

"What?" I said looking at him sideways. I wasn't convinced.

"Yeah, I also take anthropology," he said.

"Anthropology?" I asked. "You're so crazy." This was one weird boy. One minute he's like a child, ditching, badmouthing school. The other he's like a scholar. He's back on my good side.

"So, what do you like to read?" I asked, turning towards him, extra interested.

"You know, about how we evolve emotionally, how we grow and develop," he said.

"What?" I said. My hand started sweating. It was like he was my soulmate.

"You mean how we learn and grow from children to adults? Or how we grow as a culture?" I asked.

He looked at me grinning, a silly grin.

"I have a theory," he said. "More of a sentiment about how we evolve by reincarnating sideways."

"More, more," I said, perking up.

"So, some cultures believe in reincarnation. You die and you're reborn in another body. That means the idea of the soul is already there. The soul can live in many bodies, one after another. The problem is you have to die before reincarnating, before occupying another body," he said.

"I follow," I said. He was getting all into it. He really studied this stuff.

"Now imagine you don't have to die to reincarnate. You just do it every couple of years, or even every night," he explained with his hands.

"So how can you reincarnate if you don't die?" I asked.

"OK it's not really reincarnation. It's more like switching bodies. You go to another body with your soul while both are still alive," he said.

"I understand, but why?" I asked. "What would be the purpose of migrating bodies?"

He grinned and nodded. Did he like my question? "Evolution!" he said. "Evolution of the soul. This is a fast track for spiritual growth."

Boyfriend is weird. One minute he's a criminal mastermind skipping class like James Bond. The next

48

minute he's a religious scholar. I was falling a little in love with him—thank the goddess he couldn't read my mind.

"Our body remembers our lineal memories. The normal memory. What you did yesterday, your parents, or your favorite food," he added. "Our soul can't remember those lineal memories. It would be overload remembering from ten, or twenty, or one hundred lives. It would also be confusing. Can you imagine remembering forty mothers? The soul can only remember lessons, and mistakes, so we don't repeat them. I can remember feelings because I think I've had practice."

"So, you've traveled sideways?" I asked.

"You think I'm silly," he said, a side frown creeping in. He crossed his arms.

Don't let go of my hand. "No, no, I don't" I said, trying to be serious. A weird feeling came over me. As if I've had this conversation before. As if I remembered his smell, or his energy, or as if I loved him.

"Yes, I think I've done it hundreds of times," he said.

"Hundreds? Can you remember something?" I asked.

"I can remember you," he said with a magical sparkle in his eye.

49

Butterflies! I blushed again, looking down at my feet in the water.

He reached out and touched my chin, finding my eyes. "Not your face, or your voice, but your feeling. I can remember how you feel," he told me.

"How do you know how I feel? You haven't even touched me," I said.

"I remember it's you," he said digging deeper into my eyes, scooting closer, leaning in. I felt his fingertips brush ever so gently against my shoulder. Goosebumps!

"Mr. Monkey, are you trying to impress me?" I asked.

"Well yes, but that's another story," he said, swallowing hard. He paused, got serious. Took a deep breath. Maybe looking for courage?

He took my hand. *Kiss me, stupid boy.* His soft eyes defused me. My heart betrayed me with its drumming, the beat getting faster and faster. Kiss me, stupid boy. I slowly ran my tongue between my lips, closing my eyes in hopeful anticipation.

The gate to the pool opened with a squeak. It's the worst sound I've ever heard in my entire life. My Mom appeared with a polite smile. Fuck, fuck, fuck! "It's time to go kids, it's getting late," she said. He nervously jumped up to his feet, eyes wide open. Fuck, I wasn't a pumpkin! She stole my kiss. I looked at my watch; It was midnight.

I got up and shot my Mom the dirtiest look, She smiled politely at us. How can she do this to me? We obeyed and followed Mom, trailing ten feet behind, holding hands, dragging our feet like anchors all the way back to the apartment. "Two minutes," Mom said before going back inside. "Ten minutes," I quickly retorted. She gave me an evil eye. I've seen it before. "Five minutes," she said looking serious, raising five fingers, then she entered the apartment.

I faced him. "Charmed," I said smiling, hands in my pockets, mouth dry.

He looked at me shrugging. I could tell he was nervous. He said nothing. "I have to go in," I said in agony. The night was still hot, dry, and I was damp with sweat, radiating heat.

He took one step forward, standing on his toes. He waited. I didn't blink. I didn't move. Kiss me, stupid boy! He closed his eyes and leaned forward, placing one gentle hand on my elbow. His palm was sweaty. Butterflies started flopping in my stomach. I closed my eyes. He pressed his chapped lips into mine. I didn't put up a fight.

51

It was gentle, it was slow. I felt my long eyelashes brushing on his. I lost my breath. My body felt tingly, glittery, magical. He pulled away ever so slowly, as if he didn't want to lose the magic all at once. He took a step back. *Don't!* His eyes effervescent, or maybe it was my imagination. I knew those eyes. I knew that kiss.

He took another step back, looking me up and down in one long brush stroke. This wasn't an innocent look. I gulped. He walked away. My knees got a little wobbly.

I wasn't breathing. I took a deep breath. I wasn't sure what those eyes were thinking, but I knew it was dirty. He took another step back and walked away without a word. Maybe I hypnotized him. He looked back and stumbled. Adorable!

I went inside the apartment "Did he kiss you?" My Mom was standing right there.

"Mom, were you spying on me?" I complained.

"Yes, I was," she grinned.

"You know he did," I said, smiling. She smiled back following with a motherly hug. "OK go to bed, it's late. We'll talk in the morning."

"OK Mom."

"Take off the make-up before you go to bed," she said.

I went to my room and sat on the bed for a moment. I went over the kiss over and over for a few minutes. I then got up and rummaged through my drawer to find my PJs. The sexy ones. Soft, skimpy and short. If he could see me in these. I didn't take off the make-up. I picked up the mirror to see how I looked. My lipstick was smudged. I grinned like a crazy person. Is this what love felt like? It must be. I still felt butterflies in my stomach. I felt the adrenaline tickling all over my body. What, am I supposed to go to sleep now?

I went back to my bed and crossed my legs like Buddha. I wanted to be a bad girl right now— I definitely didn't want to sleep. What if I closed my eyes and went to another body? The floor fan was humming in a rhythm. It looked at me, then it looked away. Was he thinking about me? Was he thinking about the kiss?

Something was different. My body felt weird. I knew this boy. Maybe we met in another body, in another time or another life. Maybe we were meant to be together. *He's like, my lover.* I closed my eyes and imagined him kissing me. Touching me. His hot breath on my neck. "Oh my." I opened my eyes and looked at the door. Had I locked it? I didn't want Mom walking in on me. I stood and locked the door. Then got back in bed with my favorite fluffy pillow named Patricia. Yes. I named my pillows. Don't judge.

"Where was I? Oh yes." I closed my eyes again. I imagined him sneaking into my bedroom through the window. I opened my eyes and reached to unlock the window just in case. Wishful thinking. I imagined us sitting on my shaggy rug. "I love you," he tells me kissing me gently. He runs his fingers through my exposed ribs playing them like a harp. I tense but relax quickly. "Oh my." The tingly sensation returned, but lower. I reached down to touch it.

I should sneak out and go get him. If I went to sleep, then it could be over. I was just being silly. Loverboy is just crazy, and crazy contagious, probably through saliva. He gave me some of his craziness with his kiss.

I wonder if he's sleeping. I bet he's thinking of me. Of my legs. Or, yes, he's always staring at me, at my body. One minute he's mumbling like a boy, next minute he's eating me alive. I know what's on his mind.

This night can't end. We'll lose each other again. But I was so tired. My body was melting into my bed. *No, get up.* My body didn't listen. My eyes got heavy. *Get up, go get him.* Something stirred inside me. My eyes drooped, they blinked a very long blink. I'd just close my eyes for a second. Then I'd go get him.

I closed my eyes once, twice… gone.

Chapter 5: Sneaking Out

Monkey

Clink, clink. I heard a faint noise. Probably nothing. *Clink, clink.* the same noise coming from the window next to the door. I jumped out of my sleeping bag to see Alma waving, smiling behind the curtain. I had to put on some pants immediately, so I quickly closed the curtain. I searched for my shorts in the dark as quickly and as quietly as I could, slipping into my tennis shoes without socks and leaving the same t-shirt on. I paused to smell my armpits. Not so bad.

Alma opened the screen door slowly, and I stepped out. She signaled me to follow her. She reached down to pick up an extra-large shoe box and a camping lantern from the floor and started walking. I walked behind her.

We walked for close to a minute in silence. Alma was barefoot, wearing her summer pajamas. Skimpy thin lacy shorts of my favorite color, purple, with a matching top that hung from her naked shoulders with only two small strings. I could see her legs, I could see her shoulders, her stomach and the fact that she had no bra.

"Is it you, Monkey?" Alma asked.

"Yes, it's me," I said.

"Did you go to sleep?" Alma asked.

"No," I said.

"Thinking of me?" Alma said.

I kept silent, not knowing how to answer.

"Yes or no?" Alma asked. "We only have one night, you know. We might change lives tonight."

"Yes, I was thinking of you," I said. Continuing our stroll, the moon following us like a chaperon.

"Me too," said Alma. "I didn't want to take any chances just in case you're right. So, I didn't go to sleep."

"So, what's in the box?" I asked.

"You'll see when we get there," Alma said. She got close, bumping me with her hips. A soft fragrance filled me. It was a light lavender scent. She smelled of my fondest memory.

"Are you wearing perfume?" I asked. I should have sprayed some cologne.

"Please!" Alma said. "Well, maybe a little." She gave me her naughty thin smile and stopped walking to face me. "After all, I'm trying to seduce you."

I looked down from her eyes to her neck, her collarbone, then her chest under the almost transparent top, stared at her round hips below her tiny waist. I wanted to touch them but didn't know how.

"Eyes up here Monkey," Alma said, pushing my forehead with her index finger. "Come on." She jerked my arm.

"Where are we going?" I asked.

"To set a memory," Alma said.

"To set a memory?" I said.

"Yes. To set a memory. One of the ones you talked about. The one you know you remember but don't know from where. We'll anchor it so we can remember it forever. We'll store it in your great heaven library and burn it in our unforgettable soul, your alma."

"You're crazy," I said.

"No Monkey, you're crazy." Alma said. "I just got the crazy from you. I think you bit me when I wasn't looking or something."

"No, I didn't" I said.

"But you want to," Alma said with her usual wit.

"No, I don't," I lied. I actually thought about biting her several times. I've never felt that before. I fantasized about gently biting her collarbone or gnawing on her hip bone. All day I wished of taking a bite of her broad freckled shoulders.

"I know I want to bite into those abs," she confessed.

I'm sure I blushed. I could feel my cheeks going red. Good thing it was night time.

"Let me see them," Alma said.

"What?" I said.

She took a step towards me, pressing her hand against my stomach. I instinctively recoiled.

"Come on, I'm not going to rape you," Alma said. "I just want to feel your abs." She placed her box and lantern on the floor.

I straightened as she pressed her hand again. "Can I see?" She raised her eyes to meet mine.

I said nothing. I didn't know what to say. Nobody had ever asked me if they could see my stomach.

With no answer, she smiled and lifted my t-shirt just below my chest. She then held my t-shirt with her right hand and ran her left hand up and down my stomach.

"Nice," she said. "Next time I'll take a bite," Alma laughed. "Do you want to grab something?" she asked before she jerked my arm to keep on walking.

It was probably three in the morning, and I was in way over my head.

"Yes, you say?" She smiled. "Like what?" She placed one hand on her hip.

"Decisions, decisions," I said staring.

"You're a perv," Alma said and pulled me to keep walking.

We kept strolling away from the apartments. The night was hot and I could feel large drops of sweat rolling down my arms and legs. My t-shirt was sticky. I looked at Alma. Her top stuck to her chest. The night just got hotter.

We reached a solitary playground at the end of the apartment complex. It had a large playhouse in the middle. Alma smiled as she swaggered into the small shack. We could fit standing. The wooden playhouse had one window, three small chairs, and a large beanbag. This would be the last thing I remembered.

Chapter 6: Magic Shoe Box

Monkey

"Give me the lamp," Alma said. She switched it on, hanging the dim yellow light from a small hook screwed to the ceiling.

How romantic. "Is this your hangout?" I asked.

"Yes," she said. "I come here to read when my Mom comes home. Nobody ever comes here after dark so I'm always alone. I can read, smoke, and relax."

"You smoke?" I asked.

"You're so innocent," Alma teased, placing the shoe box on one of the chairs and squatting down to open it. The shoebox was carefully lined with what looked like magazine cutouts. She took out a pack of Marlboro Light cigarettes and a tiny red lighter. She smiled at me. I was gaping down at her. I could see a lot.

"Close your mouth," said Alma. I did.

She took out one cigarette, lit it, and stood back up. Alma leaned down to take something out and looked back at me. "Close your mouth," she said, and I did.

She reached into the box and handed me a small bottle. "What is it?" I asked.

"It's a flask," she said.

"What's a flask?" I asked.

"You're so silly. Do you drink?" Alma asked dragging her cigarette.

"I've only had beer," I confessed.

Alma took a step back dropping into one of the little chairs. She crossed her giant legs as they reached out to me. Her shorts lifted a little.

"Are you just going to stand there or are you going to sit?" Alma said.

I sat down in front of her. She gently held the cigarette on her lips while she opened the flask. "Cheers," she said. "To the one memory." Alma swallowed hard and handed the flask over to me.

"What is it?" I asked.

"It's bourbon," she said.

I took a swig. It burned! *Act cool.* I took a deep breath through my nose swallowing a cough. How can people drink this stuff? She snatched the bottle from me and drank more.

Alma got out a small FM radio from her shoebox. It had a wood panel and circular dials. "I'm old school," she said.

"I see," I responded. What else did she have in the shoebox?

Alma turned the dial to a click and pulled up the antenna. Music filled the tiny room with a strong, double base funk. Alma shook her head back and forth. The third base came in after twenty seconds. A piano rift followed by a keyboard between the base. Then a guitar overlay. Alma's shoulders swiveled. Mine started swiveling with hers instinctively. A husky voice jumped out of the radio. Alma jumped up with it. It was Prince, singing Erotic City. The song's slog, sexy lyrics filled the tiny room. Alma circled her head around once, twice, hands on her hips.

"That's my favorite song," I screamed over the music, thinking of the coincidence.

"I know. It's my favorite. Like I said, old school," she said, jumping around, arms in the air, circling her hips in a belly dance that hypnotized me for a second.

"Now this is what I'm talking about," Alma said. "This is the moment I won't forget. You and I sneaking out and drinking at three in the morning." She tossed the flask back to me. I opened it, drank freely, taking my third and fourth drink and looking up at her for courage.

The music continued. It was impossible not to move, event for me. Alma invited me with her index finger to get up and dance. She grabbed my hips to loosen them up. "Relax," she said. "It's only me." She pumped up the volume. I closed my eyes and moved. She turned and pressed her back against me, reaching behind to move my legs with her hands. She turned to face me.

My gods, this girl could move.

Alma placed a soft hand around my neck. The funk continued hitting us, the base vibrating through the floor.

Alma leaned into my ear. It tickled. She whispered with the lyrics about popping the cherry.

The song ended. Alma lowered the volume. "Do you know what that means?" she asked.

"Oh yeah," I said.

"What does it mean?" Alma asked.

I stared at her. She smiled shyly.

"I feel funny," I told her, sitting down, a bit dizzy. "Funny good."

"You're a lightweight," said Alma dragging smoke off her cigarette, sitting casually on my lap.

I was in heaven.

"Do you think we'll see each other again?" Alma asked me, smoke coming out with her words.

"I don't know," I said.

"How about in another body?" Alma asked crossing her legs, throwing her hands over my shoulders.

"Absofuckinglutely," I said quickly. "I'll remember you."

"Do you like me?" Alma said, knowing the answer. I said nothing. I was already drunk. "Do you love me?" she asked. "If you do, I want you to love me in your other lives."

"I love you like a sister," I said getting my wits under me.

"No, you don't," she said. "You're in love with me. I think we were lovers in another one of our other bodies, the ones you talked about."

"You're a pervert," I said, chuckling.

Alma jumped up, hands on hips, mouth opened wide in disbelief. "You dirty little bastard," she said, flicking what was left of her cigarette straight at me.

"Ouch." The cigarette burned my arm.

"You deserve it," she said.

She fished out another cigarette as we drank the flask dry. Our chuckles turned into giggles over twenty minutes.

"You know? I do believe what I told you," I said, trying hard to be serious.

"What part?" Alma said.

"The part where we know each other and the part where we wake up in a different body," I said.

"I know you do." Alma waved her skinny arms in the air to another of my favorite songs. "I never thought about it until today. But once you told me I felt older, it's as if you told me a secret and I instantly got *déjà vu*. Like we had this conversation before. Not once, but forever."

"I've never told this to anyone before," I said.

"Yes, you have, you've told me several times. I don't remember where, but I remember I know this. You've told it to me," she said. "In our other life."

Was this the alcohol talking? Or had I really found her?

Chapter 7: The Meaning of Magic

Monkey

Alma pointed at me with her cigarette, sat back on her chair, leaned back. She looked at me sideways, smile frozen. Maybe she was finally drunk. Alma raised her hand and flicked her cigarette at me using her index finger. "What now?" I protested.

"You lied to me," she said.

"What?"

"You're only sixteen years old. What the fuck!" Alma said.

"I'm practically seventeen," I said.

"Oh yes, you're a man now," Alma said.

"How did you find out?" I asked.

"Your aunt told my mom, dummy," she said.

"Ahh," I nodded.

"You know girls mature faster than boys, right? So, it's like I'm five years older than you. You're like a boy and I'm a woman," Alma said. "I could go to jail for being here with you."

"Ha, ha," I laughed. "Please."

"I'm serious," she said.

"Yeah, because you're so mature you can pretend to be twenty years old?" Alma tried to kick me from her seat but was too far.

"Are you mad at me?" I asked.

"Yes, I'm mad. You lied to me," she said, going back to being serious.

"But if I had told you my age you would've ignored me," I protested.

"I'm not that shallow," she said. "I would have noticed you're smart and, well, you're easy on the eyes. OK maybe I'm a bit shallow." She smiled and bit her lip. I liked that.

Music continued on the radio. A newer song.

"Hey, let's think in lives not in years. I'm probably much older than you. Maybe by a hundred lives and ten thousand experiences," I said.

Her glaze was suspicious. "Yes?" Alma asked.

"You know what's the funny part? We talk about how time shifts sideways. Going from life to life even in our own timeline. How about not?" I paused to think.

"Not what?" Alma asked.

"Not shifting sideways, or backwards, or to our next life. Let's just stay in this one for a while. I'm kind of liking this one," I said. "I love your freckles," I added out of nowhere. Alma smiled and touched the freckled bridge of her nose. She moved her chair a bit closer to reach me with her toes.

"Go on, Monkey," she said, opening her shoebox again.

"What else you got in there?" I asked.

"Wouldn't you like to know," she said.

"Yes, actually. It's like you can fit ten clowns in there," I said.

Alma just smiled a mischievous smile, palmed something out of the box, and slid it into her waistband. I stared at her. "What?" she said. "I'm not mad. I'm just annoyed you're so young. I love you, you know?"

"Yes, I know," I said, but I didn't.

"So, convince me you're old enough," she said.

"Old enough for what?" I said.

Her face turned mad again. Or annoyed. I couldn't tell the difference.

"I'm kidding," I said. "Don't be so sensitive."

"This is important," she said, resting her feet on my knee.

"I think you already know," I said. "I think you know I'm older than you. I'm also younger than you," I said. "It really doesn't matter. I remember you and you remember me. Now let's just forget all our sideways lives and stay here. I like it here. This feeling, this moment. It's as close as I've gotten to the meaning of life."

Alma jumped out of her chair, pulling me up with her. "You crazy Monkey, I hope you're right," she said. She took a long ballet step towards me and landed too close. Alma placed a hand on my chest. My thoughts dried up and my stomach quickly started spinning like a black hole. Her unblinking green eyes rested soft on mine. Alma grabbed my hands and moved them to her waist. Both of her large hands inched up my arms in a long, slow caress that ended with her arms stretched out over my shoulders. Goosebumps broke out over my entire body.

We danced in slow motion, shifting on one foot and then the next, eyes locked. I tried to find something in those eyes. An old friend, old memories. I found passion.

Could she hear my heart? It was banging desperately to get out of my chest. I felt the pounding on my eyes, my stomach, even on my fingertips. She got even closer, eyes wide open. Her arms relaxed, bony elbows resting on my chest. Alma looked at me. I mean, really looked at me. The look of a hundred lovers with an insatiable hunger.

Alma took half a step closer, placed her left foot in between my feet, her right foot stepping on my left one. I was sweating, sticky, short of breath. My hands felt wet over her waist. I was too excited to be embarrassed. She moved ever so gently, adjusting her hips, wiggling her knee in further between mine. I softened my knees to let her through. She was taller than me, I could feel her pelvis pushing, moving, exploring.

My insides ignited in flames. The heat stole all oxygen from my lungs, I couldn't breathe. I tightened my grip. My arms went all the way around her tiny waist. Her nose rubbed against mine. I felt her hot breath on my lips.

Alma smiled with her eyes. Licked her lips with the tip of her tongue, then licked mine. She closed her eyes. Should I close my eyes? I closed them. She pushed me and

I took two clumsy short steps backwards, stopping at the wall. We opened our eyes and smiled knowingly.

Alma pressed her entire body into me with a kiss. Her legs, stomach, chest, were so hot I could feel the radiation under my skin. She licked the inside of my teeth. Her saliva tasted of my favorite color She pulled two strings from her shoulders and pushed down her waistband, shedding all her clothes in two strokes.

The anticipation was painful. Reaching down, I got ahold and lifted her. She wrapped her long legs around me. I got to the nearest chair and sat down with her attached.

I swallowed hard, shaking with anticipation. "Yes," I whispered, feeling her. Alma claimed me, gently lifting her hips, then ever so slowly sinking them down on me, her eyes turned white. "Mmm," she murmured. A flash blinded me, I felt a jolt of electricity. I had a vision of Alma in another body—I was kissing her. As my eyes adjusted another flash blinded me and I braced for the jolt. It came with another vision. One of long ago, it came with clarity of memory. It was us, the first time we met in India. The vision dissipated as I felt my body shiver with Alma's swaying.

I looked up to see her swollen lips. Oh, her lips were made of magic. The magic of the memory you want every time you close your eyes. The memory you crave every time you wake up and before you sleep at night. Not the magic a child imagines growing up, this was real magic, the kind that tattoos your body with memory. The kind you don't forget in this lifetime, or the next. It's magic that defies the laws of time, where you don't need to breath, or speak, or move. This magic is a memory you want to drink, a passion you want to smoke. It's the magic that defines a fourteen-year-old boy. It is the meaning of life!

Time shifted sideways. I'm not sure for how long. I felt different. She felt familiar.

Alma pulled on my hair hard with one hand, gripping my neck with her other arm. She moved, oh how she moved. I felt her nails break my skin. I opened my mouth in pain, or in pleasure. She stirred quicker, tightening her grip. Alma stopped moving and her entire body pulsated. Her nails went in deeper. "Yes, Yes, Yes," she screamed and bit my lip. "Is it bleeding?" I thought I tasted blood, but she sucked it right out of my mouth, her pulsating ceasing.

Alma pulled my head back by my hair and took a casual look at me. It was a different look, primal, raw. She grinded her teeth and started swaying her hips slowly. "Again," she demanded.

My mouth opened reflexively. She closed her eyes and looked up. She moved faster. I grabbed her back and pulled her in. "Faster," I said. Alma slowed down. "Faster,"

I said. She stopped. I looked at her in disbelief, "Go on," I pleaded.

"No," Alma said.

"Please," I said.

"No," Alma said firmly. Her sweat poured on me, and through me to the floor. Her hair stuck to her body and to mine. I saw her chest expanding with every hard breath. She grinned, bearing all her teeth, "Do you want more?" she asked, panting.

"No," I said.

"Stupid Monkey," she said readjusting herself and swaying in a smooth, slow rhythm once again.

"Oh my gods," I said.

"You're delicious," Alma told me, leaning back. I felt as if we levitated. She moved slowly, then, not so much.

"More," I asked. "More." She stopped. "Please," I said. She laughed. I got up and dove into the beanbag on top of her. Alma wrapped her legs all the way around my back, pulling me in. I felt as if I was someone else. As if I knew what to do. I didn't.

"There," she said. "Right there. Please don't stop." I didn't. Our feet, legs, chest, arms contracted and expanded at the same time. "Ahhh," she screamed, gripping me even harder, squeezing my ribs with her thighs.

She softened her grip after a few seconds. We stayed paralyzed for the longest time. Tired, panting, hugging. She ever so gently backed her hips a bit. As if she didn't want to hurt me by pulling her magic away all at once. Still nose to nose, she opened her smiling, knowing eyes and tasted me on her lips blood and all. I held my breath. She glanced back at the chair. I followed her gaze. It was dripping red. She turned my head smiling shyly, blushing.

I took a long, deep breath inhaling her through my eyes. She looked very different, not like the girl of this morning, not like my friend, something had changed. Did she change? Did I change?

That was wonderful.

"That was magic," Alma whispered softly, as if she could read my mind. "Thank You."

"I Love You," I responded.

We laid next to each other exhausted, sweating. Our eyes started to close, in and out of sleep. "No," Alma said. "Don't sleep."

"It's ok," I said.

"No!" Alma said. "Please don't leave me." Tears coming out all at once.

I smiled. "We can't stay awake forever," I said. "I'll find you."

"No! I want to remember this time," Alma said.

"I'll find you. I promise." I said, eyes heavy, I closed my eyes and saw flashes of other lives. "I can see you when I close my eyes, I can see us."

"NO, don't close your eyes," said Alma.

"It's OK," I said, "I can see the last time we touched, the last time we kissed, the last time we held hands.

Alma closed her eyes, still in my arms, drops of sweat striping her freckled body. "I can see it."

I closed my eyes again, I felt a tingly sensation, as if a slight jolt of electricity went from the top of my head to my toes, then back. It didn't hurt, but it was super weird. Alma jerked. "Did you feel that?" she said.

"Absolutely," I said.

The tingling continued, I think the energy was traveling in and out of one and then the other through both of us as some sort of current.

"Please don't wait another hundred lives," Alma said, "I couldn't bear it."

My eyes filled with tears and overflowed. Alma fought, her eyes surrendering in betrayal. One short blink followed by a longer one. Gently, slowly, we blinked again, longer and longer...

Once, twice, gone...

"Will I see you again?"

Chapter 8: Déjà vu

Alma?

I felt frozen from the inside out, could not feel my fingers, could not move my eyes. I called out for him. "Monkey," I tried to scream as loud as I could, but my jaw wouldn't move. I felt a jolt of electricity and felt my body pulling away, fast, like in triple fast forward. I felt a flash of white light in my eyes and then a jerk, similar to a speeding roller-coaster ride.

I landed abruptly on my feet but felt paralyzed. My ears were ringing, my vision was dazed. I stumbled, little faint. I blinked hard to get my vision back. I saw silhouettes of people walking about around me. I heard them buzzing around. Slowly my vision started clearing. A woman walked by me, then another. Another stopped in front of me, her mouth moved, but I heard nothing but ringing. Where am I?

I blinked hard again, shapes started to clear, sounds were vibrant. What was this commotion? A dozen ladies draped in silk fussing over me in a language I didn't understand. They presented me silk garments and lavish jewelry, pointing at it and speaking incoherently. I looked around again and took a tentative step, fearing I would fall on my face. Nothing happened, so I took another step, and another. What was this awesome place? I was in a room I did not recognize. This was the largest bedroom I had ever seen. I looked around, amazed. The ceiling was painted with a night view of the sky, planets, stars and galaxies looking down at us.

I looked down to see naked breasts and gasped, attempting to cover them. My hands weren't big enough. I looked up to see a woman, she didn't even notice my body. I looked down and back, I was completely naked, in a body nothing like my own. My skin glowed in a dark bronze, the complete opposite to my super white freckled skin. I ran a hand over it to make sure it wasn't paint, then reached back and grabbed a handful of hair. It was black, soft, and covered my butt. I looked around to see if anyone was paying attention to what was happening to me, but the women briskly went about their business.

A young woman approached, presenting me with another dress. She extended her arms. I reached to feel the fabric. "So soft," I said. She responded, but it was all gibberish. I kept observing her, she looked familiar. Her soft skin and giant innocent eyes made it difficult to pin her age.

"Samyukta, how about this one?" she asked. I understood.

"Oh, my gods, I understand," I said, shocked.

"Yes, yes, congratulations," she said bobbing her head up and down and to the sides. "Samyukta, you're being childish. You need to pick a dress now," she said.

"Not that one," said another voice. An older woman walked between us, taking the dress away and exiting to another room.

I looked down to see my bare feet standing on a beautiful colorful stoned floor. Rugs and colorful fabrics with amazing patterns decorated the walls of the room. Was this my room? I turned slowly to absorb it all. There was a large open space, as if an entire wall of the room was missing. The room continued outside, furnished with sofas and lounge chairs covered with colorful fabrics. The sun was bright out and I so much wanted to feel it in my true body. I walked outside, feeling the intense sun, the humidity hit me and I started sweating. I opened my arms taking the deepest breath. "I'm home," I thought, when suddenly two women carried me by my arms. "No, no, Princess, they will see you out here," they said, rushing me inside.

"How about this one?" The woman with the dresses was back, shoving yet another silk dress into my arms. This one was deep red with emerald green accents. I took it from her arms, unfolded it and placed against my body, "How does it look?" I asked. She just bobbed her head some more. I turned around to the busy ants. "How does it look? Is it too red?" All the woman stopped their cleaning and fussing for a moment and looked at me, then continued cleaning and fussing. Another woman brought a large, elongated mirror decorated with large blue stones. She set it in front of me. I tried to slip the dress on, but the woman immediately stepped in to put it on for me. Another woman pinched the dress from behind, the dress tightened on my breast, waist and hips, revealing an hourglass figure that could make any man, or woman, blush. Another woman quickly hung large gold earrings on my ears as another slipped not one, not two or three, but five bracelets on each of my arms. All had different gemstones in blue, red, and green hues. Another lady forced a two-inch gold bracelet all the way up to my tricep.

Someone placed a chair behind me. "Sit," she said pulling me down. She then started combing my hair. Another woman in a purple long dress kneeled in front of me to apply eye liner. "Ouch," I said as she pulled my hair.

"Stay still or I'll poke your eye," said the woman in front of me.

I still had the feeling of belonging, but not really belonging. This was me, but it wasn't. "Your mother is coming," a young lady ran in announcing. An older woman with an ornate silver and green dress strolled into the room as if she owned the place. The entire colony of worker ants stopped at the same time, then rushed to stand in a straight line.

The woman walked towards me and held both my hands. "My dear, you look juicy as a strawberry in that dress," she said. "Get your sandals, we're late." One of the handmaidens moved quickly and placed emerald decorated sandals in front of my feet.

The older woman held my hand, walking me out of the room and through a long, wide hallway decorated with tapestries. We exited the building and strolled through a huge courtyard filled with fountains and gardens decorated with yellow, orange, violet and red vibrant flowers. I was already sweating, feeling the humidity over, around, and even under my dress. "We're late," said Mother, pulling me to walk faster. We rushed for ten minutes before entering another large building where a tall, skinny woman was waiting by the door.

"Head Priestess," my mother said while bowing her head.

"Sister," said the Priestess, teeth grinding. "Follow me," she said, ignoring me completely. I looked at Mother, swho signaled to follow the woman.

We entered the building and headed to cozy, medium sized room. We all sat on a rug filled with purple and green cushions arranged in a small circle. There was a silver tea set in the middle of the rug, and a servant filled our cups. My aunt, the Priestess, was still stoned faced. She signaled the servant to leave.

"You disobeyed," the Priestess blurted out, pointing a finger directly at me. I thought she would poke me in the forehead.

"What?" I asked, confused. I had just gotten here!

"She disobeyed," she said throwing her hands up, looking at Mother.

"It is that boy, that hoodlum," said the Priestess, "the gods are angry, Durga Devi is angry. She, well, she, I could not stop her," she said sobbing.

"Sister, calm down," exclaimed Mother, "tell us what happened."

The Priestess broke down crying uncontrollably. She tried to speak but could not even get a single word out. Mother moved next to her and placed my aunt's head on her shoulder. "Baby Sister, everything will be in order."

"No," sobbed my aunt, "no."

I didn't know what was happening. My tears leaked out. Did I do something wrong? Was I Samyukta? Did she do something? I still felt like a spectator in a borrowed story.

"Tell us what to do, how can we remedy this?" Mother said. "She's just a girl." She reached for my hand, I gave it to her.

"It is too late," said my aunt. "Samyukta has angered the goddess Durga Devi when she made a hole in Dharma, the divine cosmic order. It is a horribly grave offense."

"Just tell us what to do," said Mother, "she's just a girl. She's not trained, she needs to learn about the ways of the Brahmins, our priest caste."

"I am sorry, my dearest sister," said my aunt.

"What will the goddess do?" said Mother.

"She already did," said the Priestess, "Durga Devi is furious. She cursed your daughter in this life, in the next, and for all eternity."

Mother took a trembling hand to her mouth. "We must pray to her at once, we must beg for forgiveness," she shouted between sobs.

"It is too late now," said the Priestess, "the curse is already conjured to stop further damage…"

"What must we do?" said Mother, getting on her knees.

My aunt searched for her composure. "The goddess Durga Devi demands patronage from our Brahmins caste," explained my aunt, standing up tall.

"Yes, whatever, we must, we will," said Mother, standing next to my aunt, pulling me up. "We will visit her temple instantly. What must we do?"

"She wants her," Aunt gestured at me with an open hand.

"What!?" Mother shook her head. "No, she will not have her. Never!"

"And the boy," I asked.

"Prithviraj Chauhan is a commoner, a laborer. The goddess doesn't stain herself with those of the Sudras, a much lower caste," said the Priestess.

"What will happen to him?" I asked.

"He's already dead," said the Priestess with a flick of her hand.

"No!" I cried. A ring of ice traveled from my neck down my spine. "What is happening?" I said.

"The goddess cursed you and the boy never to reincarnate," said the Priestess. "Your souls will never join our ancestors, instead they will wander in nothingness.

Durga Devi will erase your memories so you will carry nothing with you through the emptiness."

"How can she do such a thing?" asked Mother. "How can she demand repayment for eternity?"

My aunt started crying again. "She wants her now," she said.

"What?" asked Mother.

"Your daughter is with child," blurted my aunt. "It is an abomination, Durga Devi wants her sacrificed before nightfall."

"With child?" cried Mother grabbing me by the shoulders.

I was as surprised as them. I couldn't speak. "What's happening?" I said, holding my tummy. I want to go back now."

"Hello, my loves," we turned to see who was there. Nobody. "I will not allow this to happen," said a sweet voice. We turned left and right, but could see nothing. "Durga Devi is an ogre, only worried about her senseless cosmic order. Everything needs to be inside the line with her." An exceptionally tall woman stepped out of the shadows. Aunt and Mother quickly dropped to their knees and placed their heads on the rug in front of them. I flinched for a second, then followed their example.

"Oh please," said the young woman. "None of that, stand up now."

The Priestess raised her head but stayed kneeling. "What may we do to deserve your presence, your divine Rati, goddess of love and..."

"How about some of that tea?" the young woman replied, cutting off my aunt.

"Yes, please, of course," said the Priestess.

The woman came closer. She was two heads taller than me, with giant almond shaped eyes and the skin of a deeply tanned angel. She sat down on the floor next to us, crossing her legs in lotus, and sipped her tea. We all sat around her. I was amazed, couldn't stop looking at her. I wanted to be her. The other two looked awestricken.

"My loves, I tried to reverse this ridiculous curse," said Rati, "but could not do it completely. This was not just a terrible act against your caste—Durga Devi is declaring war on me." She smiled with perfect teeth and continued sipping tea from the silver cup that looked tiny in her hand. "Love is not always about order," said goddess Rati. "Love is about disorder, about exploring, love can be created from nothing, with no cosmic dust and without the kiss of a goddess. This scares Durga Devi, this is why she is an old troll, this is why she has done this.

We all sat silently, not moving. "I did manage to poke a giant hole in Durga Devi's plan," said Rati, flashing her pearly teeth once again. "Samyukta will not wander in nothingness." She smiled at me and I blushed. "I couldn't completely dissolve her curse, but I managed to give your soul an opportunity to evolve, while at the same time allowing you to find your lover." I blushed again at that. "You will travel from body to body looking for Prithviraj every single day. Every night when your host body sleeps, your souls will leave and find another, and another, until the lovers can find each other. Yes, this will happen every few thousand nights, but love, with a slight push from my hand, will guide your soul. Once you find each other you will only have one day to recognize who you are and fall in love again, for the next day you will be strangers again, until the next encounter."

I felt nauseous. My body started shifting sideways, as if something was pulling me to the left. "Do not resist," said Rati. I looked at her, she took a sip of tea and winked. The pull was stronger, I was paralyzed. "Until next time, love," said Rati, as I was pulled back into my body, into my time.

+ The End of Volume 1 +

First Summer Romance

Here is a couple of more Secret Chapters

Thank You So Much

I so much appreciate you. If you like the story, there is more. For starters, you can read the deleted secret chapters for free. You can also ready the other volumes on this series and my other books.

To get the secret chapters simply download them free at www.OlsonJS.com/secret

You can also follow me on Instagram at OlsonJS

See you in Butterflyland

Olson J. S.

www.ingramcontent.com/pod-product-compliance
Lightning Source LLC
Chambersburg PA
CBHW071340130626
46556CB00004B/1956